THE LEDGE

Lesley Choyce

orca soundings

ORCA BOOK PUBLISHERS

Library and Archives Canada Cataloguing in Publication

Title: The ledge / Lesley Choyce.
Names: Choyce, Lesley, 1951– author.
Series: Orca soundings.
Description: Series statement: Orca soundings

Identifiers: Canadiana (print) 201901690IX | Canadiana (ebook) 20190169028 |
ISBN 9781459824614 (softcover) | ISBN 9781459824621 (PDF) |
ISBN 9781459824638 (EPUB)

Classification: LCC PS8555.H668 L43 2020 | DDC jc813/.54—dc23

Library of Congress Control Number: 2019943968
Simultaneously published in Canada and the United States in 2020

Summary: In this high-interest novel for teen readers, sixteen-year-old Nick tries
to adjust to his new reality after a surfing accident leaves him paralyzed.

*Orca Book Publishers is committed to reducing the consumption
of nonrenewable resources in the making of our books. We make
every effort to use materials that support a sustainable future.*

Orca Book Publishers gratefully acknowledges the support for its
publishing programs provided by the following agencies: the Government of
Canada, the Canada Council for the Arts and the Province of British Columbia
through the BC Arts Council and the Book Publishing Tax Credit.

Edited by Tanya Trafford
Design by Ella Collier
Cover images by gettyimages.ca/edb3_16 (front) and
Shutterstock.com/Krasovski Dmitri (back)

ORCA BOOK PUBLISHERS
orcabook.com

Printed and bound in Canada.

23 22 21 20 • 4 3 2 1

Chapter One

One day you're this. The next day you're that. Everything can change so quickly. Not even in just one day, but in one hour. Or, in my case, one minute. Think of it as Nick Peterson Before. And Nick Peterson After.

By the time I hit sixteen, surfing had become the biggest thing in my life. All that kid glory from skateboarding was behind me. Hockey had me for a while, but it faded. As did football and track. I had some glory there too. But it was all in the past when surfing became my thing. *The* thing. But enough ancient history. Let's cut to the event.

September found me back in school, a ripping summer of waves behind me. I had surfed almost every day. I'd given lessons, too, and made decent cash. I had persuaded Olivia to be my girl-friend. Olivia—a year older than me, with her own car and her own credit card, and willing to foot the bill for whatever we did. She resented surfing sometimes, as it took time away from her. But she knew that if she asked me to choose between her (and her car and her credit card) and surfing, surfing would win.

Being stuck sitting in a classroom sucked more than ever that year. Fall brought bigger swells out of the south.

Waves not ridden. Time wasted at a desk, not on a board. I'd been watching this place out of town, a headland called Delbert Point at the end of Fraser Road. No wave had broken there all summer. "Swell not big enough," the Wreck had once told me. The Wreck was what we all called this old guy who lived out near the point. "Need a big push out of the south," he said. He liked to talk about his glory days on the waves. I wasn't even sure I believed the stories at first. Especially the ones about the break there, the one he simply called the Ledge.

A ledge—what surfers sometimes call a slab—is a big, flat piece of rock under the surface of the ocean. A wave, but it has to be a big wave, rolls in, hits it and jacks up like double overhead in a split second. You have to hit it just right. And then this big thick monster of a thing roars over it, not acting like any sane wave you'd ever known. Thick and meaty and heavy, heavy, heavy.

If you could take off just right, you could drop, pull a power turn, set your track really high and boot it through an ugly but oh-so-hollow pocket and out the other side. If it could be done, then I figured I could do it. I was sure of it.

Of course, if the crashing lip of water hit you, you'd be squashed like a bug in the shallow water barely covering the wide black slab. Dangerous, yes?

Dangerous but doable.

So that's how it came to be that on that fateful second day of October, I was not sitting as usual in my English class, dreaming of the perfect wave.

Let me paint the picture. Big swell out of the south. Bigger than most. The beaches were all closed. Most point breaks around were big but shapeless. When I had woken up that morning I had felt it in my bones. The Ledge was calling me. You think I was going to go to freaking school? No way.

I left the house early, my board under my arm. My parents were already off to work. I hopped on my bicycle and rode to the headland at the edge of town.

And that's when I saw it. Everything the Wreck had said was true. It was big, mean and more powerful than any wave I'd ever seen. And it looked scary as hell. I slipped into my wetsuit and paddled out.

Chapter Two

Everyone knows you're not supposed to surf alone. I told that to the people in my surfing classes. But rules like that are for beginners, I figured, not for real surfers like me. That October day I was alone. All alone staring at a most turbulent sea.

The paddle out was difficult. All kinds of strange currents were tugging my board one way and another. The sky was dark. There was a storm out there at sea somewhere generating this big swell, but here, near the coast, the wind was offshore. It would make the wave hollow and fast. After a long, hard paddle, I stopped and stared at the monster of a wave, the final one of a set of seven, pounding down on the shallow shelf of rock. I could see where I'd need to take off, where I'd need to hang high on the wall of the wave, avoiding the quick drop, aiming for the shoulder and safety.

Most all of my life, I'd been good at taking the fear that would crawl up from the back of my neck into my skull and transforming it into something else. Something that made me want to do it—whatever it was. Do it and not back down.

It took me a while to figure out where to sit as I watched wave after wave rear up, spit forward, crash down and then plow shoreward as a heaving pile of white water. Even when I thought I'd found the spot, I'd be pulled one way or another by the current. Then I figured out that I had to keep paddling my six-foot board in from the deep at a forty-five-degree angle until I arrived at the perfect takeoff spot just at the instant the wave started to jack up.

I failed to get it right at least a dozen times. Discouraged? No. Challenged? *You bet.* Pumped to the gills on adrenaline, I was going to tame this beast.

And then I saw it. The last wave of the set. Big, yeah, way big. Bigger than anything I'd ever ridden. Did fear start creeping up the back stairs of my brain? For sure. Boy on a mission beating it down? You bet.

Paddle, paddle, paddle.

Got it.

It's got me.

We can do this together, wave buddy. Throw what you got.

It threw.

As I began to drop, I pounded my back foot down on my board to make the fin lock into the water and give me a radical turn to the right. So far, so good.

And then I noticed the sound. Not the normal wave sound. Not the lip crashing or the wind rushing up the face. It was the sound of the water sucking out below in the trough, sucking out over what looked like the bare face of solid stone.

But the dark wall of water before me looked like something I understood. It was the wall of a wave, after all, a big, ugly bully of a wave, but a wave nonetheless. I was moving faster than I had ever moved on a surfboard before. And it was my wave. Mine alone.

I guess I'm stretching this out. But at the time it seemed to happen in slow motion, just like in the movies. It probably all happened real quick. And real bad.

The wave changed. It got fatter. It got weirder. The hollow tube I was looking for was not round or almond-shaped. It was almost square. No lie. As the wave sucked out over the Ledge, it created this square prison that would not let me out. I had miscalculated.

What's worse is that this suddenly morphing wave collapsed completely all at once, top to bottom, with me inside. It had lured me into its mouth and then chomped down hard. It had no intention of letting me out.

I felt the weight of the water over-head slam down on me, knocking me off my board. Then I felt the rock. I hit it once, twice, and then, as blackness set in, the force of the breaking wave started pushing me off the Ledge and down into deeper water. I only felt pain for maybe a second. Then nothing.

Nothing until I woke up in an ambulance and heard the sound of the siren. I had to throw up, so I tried to lean over but couldn't. Instead I vomited straight up in the air, and it came down on my face. A woman's hand was wiping it away and sticking fingers in my mouth to remove the crud. I would have thought it was maybe the worst feeling in my life just then if it wasn't for the pain in my skull.

But even that wasn't the worst of it. I couldn't feel my legs. I couldn't move my feet.

"Don't try to move," the woman's voice said. "You had an accident."

I was still sloshing puke around in my mouth, and I wanted to say something or scream something, but it just took too much energy.

So I lay there in unbelievable pain, looking up at the lights in the ceiling. I desperately tried to remember what had happened in those seconds after the wave slammed me into the rocky bottom.

Somehow I had ended up onshore and ultimately here in a wailing ambulance on its way to the hospital.

Chapter Three

I could report to you a whole lot of
boring bullshit that happened during the
next month. But I'll give you the short
version.

I couldn't move my legs.

The doctors said I might recover the
feeling in my legs and walk again. Or
I might not.

My parents freaked out.

I freaked out.

Shrinks started coaching me about my "new situation."

A guy named Ahmad became my physical therapist and kept telling me to trust him and be patient.

I missed a month of school.

I ended up home in my bedroom with a goddamn catheter attached to my you-know-what, playing video games where the bad guys were the good guys and the good guys were the ones I was killing.

If you think I am going to drag you through all that and give you more dirt on my sad situation, then I'll say the same thing to you as I said to the kids at school when I went back. Screw you. Really. Frig off.

Oh, and get this. I returned to school in a motorized wheelchair. Yup, I did. It just kept getting better and better. But if you want the whole story of what went down between the wave and the return of the defeated warrior to the hallowed halls of high school, you'll have to ask someone else. I don't want to relive it.

In fact, maybe you could ask Olivia. She and I lasted all of two weeks after the accident. That hurt too. So maybe I should, like the shrink says, "talk and share the pain."

One day she came into my bedroom while I was propped up killing a team of FBI agents who were chasing me because I had threatened to deploy a deadly virus on Philadelphia.

"How are things today, Nick?"

"Things are about the same. Life sucks. This sucks. Each morning I wake to the same old shit. And nothing seems to change."

"I'm sorry."

"People keep saying that. But I was the one who did this to me. So I don't even have the luxury of blaming someone else." I threw the game controller at the wall, and the video game froze.

Olivia walked over to pick it up. Something about her, something in the air in the room, told me she was here to tell me something important. "Nick?" she began sweetly.

"Olivia?" Sarcasm poisoned my voice, but then, that same sarcasm had poisoned just about every word that had come out of my mouth since my big wipeout.

"I don't think I can do this," she said.

I almost laughed. Almost but not quite. "Do what?"

"I'm not strong like you."

"What's that supposed to mean?"

"It's just that…"

"Just *what*? Say it."

"It's just that it hurts me so much to see you like this."

"That makes two of us."

"But I'm not someone who's good at…" Olivia looked away from me then and walked to the window and opened the blinds. I cringed at the bright light, but it was that sunlight coming into the room that maybe allowed me to see where this was going.

I took a deep breath. She was breaking up with me. The girl was here to tell me she was moving on. The rage began to grow deep within. I almost exploded.

And then she started to cry. She sat down on the bed, leaned into me and cried until I felt her tears on my shirt. My rage subsided. I felt sorry for her. Of course she couldn't handle this. I couldn't handle this either. The only difference was that she had a choice and I didn't.

I consoled her as only a paralyzed teenage boy can console a pretty but self-centered girlfriend who is dumping him but is brave enough to come into his bedroom and say it in person instead of by text message.

I wanted to cry too, for both of us. Instead I held her in my arms, as my shirt sopped up the tears, and let her have a good healthy cry. Then she said some really silly shit like, "I'll always remember our time together" or something inane like that.

And then she left my room. It was over.

My thought that day was, A lot of things are over. Most everything in my life that I'd ever cared about was over.

✦

And then it was back to school for Mr. Motorized Man. The teachers would all find a special place in the classroom where I could park my wheelchair. Kids would sneak looks at me, thinking, Is that the same Nick Peterson who was

once quarterback of the football team?
Is that the Nick Peterson who was on
the cover of *Thrasher* magazine when
he was, like, thirteen?

Chapter Four

So now you have a pretty clear picture of Nick Before and Nick After. If you want a list of the things I missed most—from peeing on my own to surfing overhead walls of glass for three hours straight—it would take too long. I should just get on with the story.

I liked the drugs. The painkillers. The pain dwindled—the physical pain, that is.

Hey, I still couldn't really feel much of anything from the waist down. Lucky me. But I told the docs that I was still in pain so they would keep the meds coming. I was legally buzzed and occasionally blitzed if I took more than the recommended dose. But the drugs were making me dull. It was hard to concentrate in school. Hard even to concentrate on the video games sometimes. At least I didn't have to put any energy or thought into keeping up with a relationship.

Dreams about that wave kept coming back to haunt me. Night after night. My parents kept referring to it as "the accident," as did most everyone else. But it wasn't an accident. It was my own doing. And that made it all seem even worse.

Ahmad gave me some stupid books to read by people who had recovered from cancer or car accidents or sports injuries. The ones who tell you that you can grow and learn from bad things in life and become a more fully realized person. In my video-game world, I imagined I was hunting down those stupid optimists and blasting them from the face of the earth.

But Ahmad was good to me. I gave him a hard time, and he always took my crap. He'd been assigned to me right after I ended up in the hospital. I gave him so much shit he should have thrown me down a flight of stairs and finished off the job. But he never lost his cool with me. Instead he just smiled. At first I hated that smile.

And then I noticed that he was the only one who wasn't giving me a smile filled with pity.

"I am here to help you the best way I can," he told me. "Yes, they pay me to do this," he had replied after I hurled an insulting comeback about it just being his job. "And I'm grateful," he'd added.

But I could tell it wasn't just the pay.

I never asked him about himself until after Olivia dumped me. "Ahmad, you're not from around here, are you?"

"Everyone asks that. No. I'm from far away."

"How far away?"

"The Middle East. Syria."

"Any surf in Syria?"

He smiled. "I think so. Around Latakia. You know, usually when I name that country, people have opinions they seem to need to share."

"Ever surf?"

"No. I'm not good at things like that. No good balance. Besides, I hear surfing can be dangerous." There was just a hint of another kind of smile. A devilish smile.

"No," I said. "Surfing's really pretty safe unless you're an idiot like me."

"Maybe you could give me a lesson sometime."

"Maybe," I said. And that's when it occurred to me. This was the first honest guy-to-guy conversation I'd had with anyone since "the event."

We had a lot more conversations. I was into week six of my three-times-a-week physio sessions with Ahmad when I decided he was my only true ally in the world now. I mean, my parents were my parents, and teachers tried to be nice, and some kids tried to be kind to the gimp in the wheelchair who had once tossed a mighty mean football. But Ahmad was the real thing.

Even though I kept dreaming about that damn wave, I didn't really remember the actual event. The only memory I had was of the paddle out, the drop, the monster pitching over me and then nothing. Truly nothing at all. How the hell did I end up out of the water? How did I survive? In the morning I'd pop a few more of those pills and watch helplessly as my mom or my dad got me ready. Then my dad would drive me to school in the used van he had bought, the one with the lift. He'd had to sell the Subaru he loved so he could buy it. I felt kind of guilty about that.

One night, after downing a few more of the pills than I should have, I had a nice little buzz going, like the one that got me through morning classes at school. I didn't want to go to sleep. I made the mistake of calling Olivia.

I think she'd been smoking weed. She had the dreamy-sounding voice that used to seem so sexy to me. But I heard someone cough in the background. She wasn't alone.

"Nick," she said. "I was just thinking of you. So cool that you called."

"I just wanted to hear your voice," I said like a fool. "I miss you." As soon as the words were out, I knew this was bad. Bad and getting worse. I heard how weak and pitiful I sounded.

"I miss you too," she said. I knew she was lying. And there was that cough again.

"I miss us," I continued. "I miss doing things with you." This was all true, but as soon as I'd said it, I knew it wasn't like we'd had this great romantic thing going. To be honest, I think we had fallen in together because we looked oh so cool as a pair. Mr. and Ms. Universe—or, at least, the high-school version. Truth is, I think we used each other. We liked the way kids looked at us when we were together. The perfect couple. Beauty and the Buff—that would be me. Now it would be more like Beauty and the Beast.

"They say I'm improving," I continued. "I should be good as new in no time." Nobody at the hospital or anywhere else had said anything like this. But I hadn't given up hope.

"I can't forgive myself for walking out on you after the accident," she said.

There was that word again. But I wanted to believe her. So this was good, right?

"Maybe we can hang out together again sometime. Sometime soon." I was pushing it. Better to leave it alone.

The pause. The damn silence of the awkward pause. Me wondering if she'd accidentally dropped her cell. Or if she was still there. Then the cough again. It was the cough of someone who'd had too big a toke of weed. Someone—some *guy*—was there with her. "Sure," she finally said. "Let me think about it and figure something out."

"Great," I said half-heartedly, knowing it would never happen, knowing it was just a way to end the conversation. "See ya in school."

"See ya."

Boom. Dumb idea calling Olivia. The girl had moved on. Who could blame her? But I was pissed. Frustrated and pissed in a way I can't fully explain. I tossed my phone in the trash can by my bed.

And then I spit on it.

Chapter Five

Days rolled by. And I do mean rolled.
Hell, I couldn't walk. So I rolled.
I started doing upper-body exercises
with some coaching from Ahmad.
I hadn't fully lost my arms—my
paddling arms. That was the good news.
I'd always been a good paddler with
strong arms that could catch any wave
I wanted. I'd weakened during the first

few weeks of recovery, but now I was getting my arms back and could feel my muscles tightening under the skin.

I think girls noticed the arms. Or, at least, I believed they did. I wore tight short-sleeve shirts to show off my biceps. Pretty low-life, right? All I needed was a pack of smokes rolled up in one sleeve. A couple of the guys complimented me, but it sounded pretty false. Rowan and Pool, comrades from my football days, started walking with me between classes. Rowan wanted to know about the wave. I didn't want to talk about it. Pool wanted to know if I could still "do it" in my current condition. I didn't want to think about sex. I didn't want to think about all the things I might never do from now on. I told them both to go to hell.

Worse were the kids who felt sorry for me and tried to be nice to me, holding open classroom doors, trying to help me with my locker or, worst of the worst, offering to carry my books. Screw them all.

Then, on one particularly dismal day when I'd had serious problems with my chair and had needed to ask for help from a teacher to deal with my catheter, I was at my locker and accidentally dumped my chemistry, math and history textbooks on the floor. It was the end of the day on Friday, and the halls were emptying. Everyone was running out the door to catch buses or hop in cars to chase off to the coffee shop or get into some kind of righteous trouble. Me, I'd be hanging back, waiting for the Accessibus to make its way here. Better for everyone to be gone anyway, so they didn't stare at me while the frigging hydraulic lift raised my chair and me up onto the bus.

I was thinking dark thoughts as I stared down at my books splayed on the shiny concrete floor. I was thinking how good it would feel to just kick the suckers as hard as I could, like in the old days when I could punt a football downfield and through the goalposts like the glory boy I was.

Then who shows up but Keira.

Keira, the ultimate twenty-first-century goth girl. Keira who used to give me dirty looks when Olivia and I walked down the hall like we owned the place. Keira of the stud-heavy ears, pierced nose and tongue, and clothes bought secondhand on Mars.

She stopped and just stood there, staring down at me. (Oh, did I say how much I hate everyone, and I mean everyone, staring *down* at me now that I am in the chair?) "You need some help, Nick?" she said, trying to sound polite.

"Not from you, girl freak," I answered.

She blinked and scrunched up her lips, making the pin in her chin stick out a little. "Really?" she said, her voice a half octave higher.

"Really. So piss off, girl freak." I don't know why I felt like I had to use that word again.

Instead of walking away, she smiled. "Nicky," she said. (And no one ever calls me Nicky except my grandmother). "How refreshing. Finally someone around here who says what they really feel. And to my face, no less." She stooped, picked up all three books and hugged them to her chest. But she didn't hand them back to me. "So," she said, "tell me what it's like exactly in your own private freakdom. I'd really like to know."

"Give me back my damn books," I said, reaching out to her, one hand involuntarily curled into a fist.

"Not until you answer."

I wasn't about to play her game. I said nothing. I stared her down.

She finally took the hint. She set the books down gently in my lap and then walked away.

✦

When the bus dropped me off at my physio appointment at the hospital, I told Ahmad about Keira. "Explain this 'freak' thing to me," he said. "I hear the expression but don't always understand how people use it."

"It's a word to describe people who are different. People who don't fit in or who try hard *not* to fit in."

"And that's bad?"

"Yeah."

Chapter Six

I think Ahmad tried hard not to feel sorry for me. He'd been claiming I was making progress, but I couldn't see it. I kept working on my arms and upper body. I was getting to the point where I could haul my near-useless body a few feet across the room with the help of the bars, but it wasn't what you could call walking.

"These things take time," Ahmad kept saying, patient as always and acting as always like I mattered. "You will get better and get stronger. I promise." But he never actually said the words I wanted him to say: *You will walk again.*

I assumed his words were empty promises, bright, positive notions said to my face to give me hope. I didn't really believe any of it. In fact, and here's the kicker, I'm not sure I wanted to believe. I mean, this hope thing. Suppose I bought into it and it turned out to be bullshit like so much else in life? Then I'd be worse off. I was thinking acceptance was more the way to go. Acceptance and meds.

If school was daily torture, late nights sitting in my room—popping a few more pills than prescribed and playing a video game, watching a movie or just listening to music—were enough to make the world go away. And I was beginning to like that more and more.

Cold days were coming on. A little snow here and there. You think winter is a pain in the ass for you, just think about what it's like when you can't move your legs and you're stuck in a motorized wheelchair. My dad was always harping on the fact that I was lucky we could afford this machine with its battery-powered motor so I could move around on my own. He was lousy at the cup-is-half-full philosophy, and he and I had grown apart a long time back, well before the accident. The man is all about business—he is a wholesaler of lawn-mower parts.

My mother had quit her job after my accident. She had been a dental hygienist who made more money than my father—which really pissed him off sometimes. But she'd quit to take care of me. She could have gone back after I started school. But she didn't.

So now lawn-mower man footed all the bills and did a fine job of complaining every time he opened another envelope that said he owed someone money. I'd asked both of them to help me figure out how I had made it ashore and into the ambulance. I wanted to know the story. I had even called the ambulance company and the hospital, hoping to fill in the gaps. But no one wanted to bother with me. The ambulance dispatcher told me that both the driver and the other paramedic on duty the day of the killer wave no longer worked for the company.

One bright, cold day in the school parking lot, as I had just gotten off the bus and was wobbling my way through the freezing slush in the parking lot, I saw this trash heap of a car pull in. Keira was behind the wheel. I saw the parking space she was aiming for right behind me, so I did a 180-degree turn right away and blocked it. I looked right at her through the windshield. She slammed on the brakes, scrunched up her face near the glass and gave me the finger.

I don't know why, but it made me smile. A big, shit-eating smile. She slammed on her horn, and all the kids slopping around in the slushy parking lot looked at us. And for once I rather liked that. I really did.

When you're center stage and liking it, there's nothing you should do but savor the moment, let it linger.

So I lingered. There's nothing quite like a guy in a wheelchair, motorized or not, just taking his time about budging when he's in someone's way.

And then the moment passed. Kids moved on, I toggled the controls and moved out of her way. She pulled in too far and bumped the front of the car into the wooden fencing. "Nice parking job," I said loud enough for her to hear.

"Screw you," she said, getting out and slamming the car door.

She looked like maybe she was having a bad morning as she stomped past me, her orange sneakers getting soaked in the dirty slush.

"Hey," I said, "I'm sorry. I was just goofing around."

"Great for you," she said, almost out of earshot already.

"No," I shouted. "I'm really sorry."

She kept walking as the wind whipped up and a few stray flakes of snow came down.

"Really sorry," I repeated at the top of my lungs.

She stopped, then started again toward the school, shaking her head. I figured I *had* been a bit of an ass about blocking the parking spot. I tried to wheel myself toward the school door but discovered I was now bogged down in the mess of snow and ice on the pavement. Great, I thought, now I'm stuck here for the day. And everyone in the school can watch me freeze to death, from the comfort of their warm classrooms.

It was then that Keira must have tuned in to my brain waves. Her hand was even on the school door when she suddenly pivoted and came stomping back toward me. I gave up on trying to get unstuck. I figured maybe she'd just tip me over and leave me there in the slush. That would look even better to my classmates.

She walked up to me and kicked the wheel of my chair.

"That all you got?" I asked.

"Smart-ass." She wasn't smiling.

"I said I'm sorry. I saw you coming. I thought you might just run me over and put me out of my misery." It was meant to be a joke.

She now looked concerned, dead serious. "You don't really mean that, do you?"

"No," I said. "Although it probably would play out a whole lot better than me sitting here like a beached whale, spinning my wheels in ice water."

"You're stuck?"

"Yes."

She yanked at the handles on the back of the chair. "Damn, this thing's heavy."

"And I forgot to put my winter tires on," I said. "Woe is me."

She wrenched my chair forward. "There." And I was free.

I looked up to focus on her as snowflakes landed on my face. I could feel them hitting my cheeks and landing on my eyelashes. I could see that Keira really looked a mess. Her hair was all crazy tangled, and she had on just a light jacket. Her sneakers were soaked through, and her tight jeans were wet almost to her knees from struggling to get me unstuck. No one else had bothered to come to assist.

And then she did something really unexpected. She brushed the snow out of my face with a gentle swish of her hand.

"I didn't know you drove," I said, wanting to say something, anything, to break the awkward silence that followed.

"I drive. But I don't have a license. I was late. My mom said I could take the car—I couldn't afford to be late again. I'm already in deep shit here. Always have been, as far back as I can remember."

"How is it?"

"How's what?"

"Being in deep shit?"

"You wouldn't know, I guess."

"Well, once upon a time in a fairy tale, no. I didn't know. Now. Well, you can probably figure it out."

"C'mon," she said. "Why don't you cut class and sit in the cafeteria with me? Once I check in with homeroom, they won't even notice. I'll find some hot water and make us some instant coffee."

"It sounds like a date," I said.

"Yeah," she said sarcastically, guiding me across the parking lot as my wheels spit more icy water onto her pant legs. "I just love first dates."

Chapter Seven

I'd skipped a lot of classes even before I became wheelchair man, and no one had given me much of a hard time. Now no teacher said anything if I skipped their class. You can get a fair bit of mileage out of pity, if you work it right.

Keira got hot water from the caf lady and brought back two disposable cups. I watched as she scooped some dark-brown crystals into the two cups from a baggie in her backpack. After she had stirred the liquid in both cups with a pencil, she held the baggie up. "Mr. Vincenzo tried to bust me for this," she said with a smile of satisfaction on her face.

"The principal tried to bust you for instant coffee?"

She continued to smile. The girl was kind of cute really. I'd never noticed.

"I was putting it into my locker. My backup stash of Maxwell House. He grabbed it and asked what it was. And I wouldn't tell him."

Of course. Just like her not to tell him it was coffee.

"When he said he'd send it to the cops to have it analyzed, I laughed so hard I nearly peed myself."

"I'm sorry to say I know exactly what that's like. He really thought it was some kind of drug?"

"I guess so. Chocolate cocaine, maybe, or something worse. He phoned my mom, and she gave him a really hard time, but she didn't tell him it was freeze-dried coffee either. The funny thing is, I never heard a word from Mr. Vincenzo again. I guess the police had a good laugh at his expense and that was that. Still, I have to watch out for him. He has my number, and he's not gonna start any fan club on my behalf." She waved what was left in the little baggie in the air for a monitor or a teacher to see.

The bell rang for second period, and I expected Keira to get up and run to her next class. She didn't. "Shouldn't we go?" I said.

She held up her cup. "I'm not finished."

"But you'll be in trouble, right?"

"Hey, I'm always in trouble." She pointed to the part-time cafeteria monitors and added, "I bet right now one of them is thinking, I want to go harass the girl talking to the gimp in a wheelchair."

"Is that what I am? A gimp?"

She gave me a stern look. "I didn't mean it in a nasty way. It's a label. Sometimes you have to work with what they sling at you. Work with it to your advantage."

"I don't know about that."

"I do," she said. "I definitely do. But you're right. I should move my ass. Gotta quiz in modern history that I need to fail. Can I call you if I get bored sometime?"

That threw me off. "Yeah, I guess. But only when you're bored."

"Touché. That's French for a good comeback. Give me your phone."

I gave her my phone, and she looked up my number. She didn't write it down. Maybe this was just a sick joke.

And then she was gone, and I was alone at my table with a really bad cup of cold instant coffee. No sugar, no milk. Just cold, black instant coffee. I sucked it back like I was downing a shot of something wicked.

Chapter Eight

Ahmad was always so patient, so professional, but he generally held back his own opinions and didn't offer up any personal information about himself. So he surprised me when he said to me one day after school, "My mother wants me to invite you to our house for Sunday dinner."

"Your mother?" I asked.

"Yes. I'm not really supposed to have informal interactions with my clients. But she says you are different."

"You live with your mother?" This struck me as weird. I guessed Ahmad to be at least in his late twenties.

"Yes. My family has stayed together, at least some of us, since we arrived." He seemed a little annoyed at my question. "So I live with my mother and little sister. She's about your age but goes to school over at West High."

"Hey, you're not trying to set me up with your sister, are you?" I joked.

He gave me a gentle smack to the head. "Definitely not. Now tell me yes or no so I can report back to my mother. And I'm warning you, she won't take no for an answer."

"No then."

"Good. I'll see you Sunday at four o'clock. I'll text you the address."

✦

I didn't know what to expect. In fact, I was more than a little nervous. I thought of taking a couple of the pills prescribed for my anxiety but decided against it. Sometimes they made me light-headed, which was okay for playing video games but not good for socializing.

My mom drove me there and made a quick exit as soon as the hellos were over at the door. "I'll pick you up whenever you call," she said. Good old mom.

This was the first time I'd seen Ahmad in clothes other than his official hospital greens. He had his hair slicked back and was wearing a boldly colored shirt. His mother, a very short woman, was wearing an equally bold scarf on her head. She walked up to me and held my face in her hands for what seemed like a long time. "Come in," she said, her dark, piercing eyes looking straight into mine. "We are honored to have you as a guest."

"Let him go, Mother," Ahmad said. "Nick came here to eat." And then he turned to me. "I hope you are hungry."

I wasn't. That was one of the downsides of my condition and sometimes the drugs. "I'm famished," I said, using a big word I'd heard in an English movie.

"Then come. Sit," Ahmad said and then slapped his head. It was the "sit" part, I guessed. Funny that even someone in his occupation would accidentally slip up.

"It's fine," I said. "Don't worry about it."

There was a clear path to the dining-room table and a place for me to tuck in. It was the strangest thing, but when I pulled up I hit my foot against a table leg. And it hurt. Ouch. It really hurt.

I felt pain in my foot. That had not happened since the accident.

I didn't have a chance to think more about it or say anything to Ahmad, because just then Ahmad's sister walked into the room, carrying two full bowls of food. "This is my sister, Eva," said Ahmad. Eva was tall and and had her mother's deep dark eyes. Her hair, not covered with a scarf, hung down to her shoulders.

I nodded a hello. Eva looked as uncomfortable as I was, maybe more. Her mother followed with more plates of food. None of it looked familiar, but I decided not to ask what anything was.

Ahmad must have realized that the dishes were all new to me, because he started pointing and naming each one. "Here," he said, leaning over and scooping different things onto my plate. "Try a bit of everything."

It all tasted strange but was really, really good. I found my appetite returning. Ahmad's mother, who insisted I call her Sidra, looked pleased that I kept shoveling in food.

"Here," said Ahmad. "You must try this on your falafel." He spooned some kind of red sauce onto my plate. "Taste," he instructed.

I dutifully tasted. It was spicy—so spicy my mouth began to burn. Whatever it was, it was hotter than any chili sauce I had ever tasted.

Everyone was clearly amused by my reaction. Eva leaned across the table and handed me a glass of water. "You should not have trusted my brother," she said with a smile. "He gave you muhammarah—a hot-pepper dish from our home. He should not have done that."

No, he shouldn't have. I couldn't speak. My nose was burning now, and my eyes were watering. Sidra could not help but laugh now. Ahmad, who'd never really given an indication of having even the slightest sense of humor, seemed quite proud of himself. As I began to recover, I realized that the pepper joke was a good thing. A kind of test. A way of saying, *You are new here, but we tease you as a way of welcoming you.*

I drank most of the water and then inched my chair a tiny bit closer to the table so I wouldn't spill any food. I hit my foot on the table leg again and felt a small amount of pain. What was that about?

Eva distracted me with questions about school—mostly ones I didn't want to answer. Her way of speaking was very formal, like Ahmad's, but she seemed genuinely interested. When there was a pause in the conversation,

I tried to keep up my end by asking about a dish I hadn't tried yet. It looked like green beans mixed with olives.

Ahmad gave me a stunned look. "You've never seen beans before? You've never seen olives?"

"Well, yeah, but—"

"But nothing. We call it beans with olives. Here," he said leaning toward me. "Try some."

I looked suspiciously at the dish he was holding out. "Uh…I'm a bit afraid to," I said.

Ahmad laughed and then made a show of asking his mother, "Have you ever seen anyone afraid of beans and olives?"

"Shush," said Sidra, turning to me. "It has garlic and lemon. Very good. You should try it."

So I did, and it was delicious. In fact, the whole meal was. I hadn't really been interested in food since—well, you know. But all these new flavors were opening a door for me.

Chapter Nine

After the main meal there were cakes and sweet tea. Eva wanted to talk to me about surfing. I think she had been prompted by Ahmad to do so. I, however, didn't want to talk about surfing or even think about it. I tried to change the subject.

"Did you all come to this country together, at the same time?" I asked.

Ahmad lowered his head. Eva looked away. Only Sidra looked straight at me as she took a deep breath. "My other son, Tariq, was killed when a missile hit his school. It was the middle of the day."

And then silence.

"I'm sorry. I didn't know," I said. "Who did this?"

She shook her head. "I don't know. We never found out. It could have been the rebels or it could have been the military. It doesn't matter now."

"No, it doesn't matter," Ahmad echoed.

I wanted to say it would have damn well mattered to me, but I knew it wasn't for me to comment on such a sensitive topic.

"We loved Tariq very much," Ahmad's mother said. "He was only twelve." I watched as her eyes teared up.

Eva noticed too and spoke to fill the silence. "Right after Tariq was killed, our father secured passage for us on a boat headed to a Greek island. From there we made our way here. He stayed behind to help others escape. We have heard from him recently. He is still in Syria but has been detained. We are hoping…" She trailed off.

"And we have a cousin," she added after a moment, obviously wanting to get off the topic of their father. "He has been injured, but his family found a way to get him to Turkey and then on a plane across the Atlantic. He is coming to live with us this week."

Ahmad took a deep breath. "Okay, Eva. I think we have burdened our guest enough for one night. Here, have some basbousa." I was full, but I somehow found room for the sweet, sticky cake.

Eva and Sidra left the room, and Ahmad poured us more tea. "Thank you for coming to dinner. Yes, my mother insisted, but I thought it would be nice for you to meet my family," he said. "I don't have many friends. We don't ever really have guests over. The other people we know who have come from Syria live far from here." He began to wheel me away from the table and into the living room. There wasn't much room to maneuver in the small house, and I banged my foot yet again, this time on a bookcase. It was my other foot, and I felt a twinge of pain as I had earlier.

"Ouch," I said.

"You felt that?" asked Ahmad.

"I felt something. It hurt."

"I have not heard you say that before."

With Ahmad's reaction, I suddenly experienced a small bubble of possibility in my brain. "Does this mean something?"

"I don't know. It might be important. I think we should do some tests. I'll call your doctor tomorrow and suggest they get right on it."

"Thank you," I said.

Chapter Ten

I felt shooting pains in both legs in bed that night. At first I thought this was a good sign, but, of course, I still couldn't move them. I just felt the pain. I took a couple pills through the night and that helped, so I took a couple more in the morning. When my mom dropped me off at school, I was in a serious fog. Not good.

Rowan and Pool were hanging out by the front door, and Rowan moved to help me get through the door. He said something to Pool, and I didn't hear it. I thought it was a crude remark about me, but I could have been wrong. I thought Pool snickered, but maybe I was just being paranoid. Once inside, my brain carried me over to the dark side. I hit my brake and wheeled around. Rowan and Pool looked startled.

"What?" Rowan asked.

"Piss off," I said. "Just piss off."

Rowan looked at Pool and then gave me a look. Pool held out his middle finger and tapped me on the cheek with it. And then they were gone. Man, I was in a rotten mood. If you can, conjure in your head a cocktail of feeling paranoid, anxious, tired, antsy and bored all at the same time. Well, that was me sitting in English class as Mr. Carlton explained how the English poets were obsessed with time and aging and how nothing stayed the same. Everything young gets old. Everything beautiful turns to something ugly. Everything living must die. Just what I needed that morning.

I wanted to stand up and shout out, *Screw you, William Shakespeare! Bugger off, John Milton! Rot in your grave, Christopher Marlowe!* But instead I closed my eyes and fell asleep. And dreamed yet again about that damn wave.

To Mr. Carlton, the dean of human mortality, I give some credit for just letting me be. I guess there was no class in his room after my English period was over, because I awoke to an empty room and more pain in my right foot. But now my chair was over by the windows.

Mr. C. was at his desk, grading papers and eating a sandwich. When he saw that I was awake, he asked, "You okay, Nick? Need to go to the nurse or something?"

"No," I said. "It's the meds. And I'm having a bad day."

"We all have bad days," he said, trying to be nice.

"Not like mine," I said.

"No," he admitted. "Not like yours." And then he changed the subject. "I guess English poetry didn't cheer you up."

"Not today," I said.

The classroom door opened right about then.

"Hi, Keira, how can I help you?" asked Mr. C.

"Don't worry—I didn't come to complain about that lousy grade you gave me last year."

Mr. C. looked a little baffled.

"I came to find Nick."

I took another deep breath and tried to clear the fog in my head.

"Let's go," she said, walking toward me and then trying to move my chair.

It didn't move at first, but I flipped off the brake and we lurched forward. Mr. Carlton watched closely, wondering, I'm sure, what was going on.

"Where are we going?" I asked as we moved to the front of the room and past Mr. C., who watched with his sandwich halfway to his mouth.

"Wherever you want," she said.

Chapter Eleven

"Let's go to the library," I said, for no particular reason.

So we went to the library. Mrs. Jenson heard us as we rolled in and, without looking up, said, "The library's closed this period." She too was eating her lunch. But then she stopped and gave us the once-over.

"We just need a quiet place to hang out," Keira said.

"Like I said, the library is closed," Mrs. Jenson repeated.

Keira kept looking at her.

"Okay," Mrs. Jenson said. "But no video games or internet noise. I need quiet too."

So I rolled toward the big wall of windows, and Keira followed. We both sat there looking out at the dead grass, the dark sky and the lifeless windows reflecting back at us from the other side of the courtyard.

I told her about my recurring dream. She listened to me talk about what I remembered of the day of the wave. It was the first time I'd talked about it in a long while, even though it had played out in my head a million times.

"Have you been back there since?"

"No."

"Maybe you should. Maybe this is all some kind of PTSD thing like what the news keeps talking about. Seems to me almost everyone on the planet is suffering from some kind of trauma disorder. Most of it sounds like bullshit to me. But maybe you have the real thing."

"Maybe. But I'm not sure that going back to the Ledge would help in any way."

"Maybe not. It was just an idea."

Then something triggered in my head. "But I do know something that would."

"What?"

"I've never been able to figure out how I got ashore, how I ended up in the ambulance. I've asked, but no one seems to know."

"Then let's figure it out."

"I've tried. The hospital staff said they didn't know. The ambulance brought me to the ER. That was it. The paramedics who took me in aren't there anymore, and the ambulance people wouldn't tell me anything."

"Bullshit. You want to know the story, and you deserve to find out. Do you think it will help?"

"Maybe."

"Why do you think you want to know so bad?"

"Because I'm pretty sure I should have died that day. I was out there alone. Not another soul around. I had sealed my own fate, like the idiot that I was."

"But you *didn't* die. And I don't think you just washed onto the beach and the paramedics showed up."

"Yeah, that doesn't make sense."

"Then let's track down the paramedics. One of them was a woman, right?"

Keira moved us to a computer terminal and punched some keys. Mrs. Jenson looked over. I thought she was going to chase us away, but she didn't. She just held a finger to her lips in the classic shush-says-the-librarian fashion.

"This isn't rocket science," Keira whispered. I watched the screen as she located the website of the hospital and followed some links to the list of private ambulance companies that served it. "Which one?"

"That one," I said, pointing to All-County Emergency Service. "But they told me they couldn't help."

"Tell me the date of your accident," she said.

"October second," I said.

She was already on her cell phone, calling the ambulance dispatch.

Chapter Twelve

Let's just say Keira didn't exactly have a good phone personality. "Let me speak to someone in charge," she snapped, clicking to speaker phone and turning the volume way down so I could listen but Jenson wouldn't kick us out.

"Is this an emergency?" a man's voice asked.

"No. I just want to speak to whoever is in charge."

"You need to give me a good reason," he said, now sounding a bit pissed.

"Don't be an asshole," Keira spit out. "Just let me speak to your boss. Please." The "please" sounded more like her traditional "screw you." But after a brief silence it got her through.

"Anderson here," said a woman's voice. "What is this about?"

"I'm working with a client," Keira said, winking at me. "His name is Nick Peterson. Your paramedics took him to the hospital back in early October. We're trying to nail down some important details about what happened that day. Part of his therapy. It's really quite important."

The woman asked for the exact date, and Keira gave it to her.

"The surfing accident, right. Give me a minute to call up a file."

So far, so good, I thought. Keira was now being civil, and the woman on the other end seemed to want to help. She came on the line again. "Landon and Becker were on call. Becker driving, and Landon must have been in the crib with Peterson. Pretty bad situation."

"Peterson is still in recovery," Keira said, sounding even more professional now. "We think that if we can piece together what happened in the water, it will help him psychologically."

"I can tell you what happened in the water. He got slam-dunked by a big wave, and he hit something underwater. *Likely a severe spinal injury*, it says here, but you probably know a lot more than that."

"We're trying to find out how he ended up on the shore and who called 9-1-1."

"It says here that whoever called 9-1-1 didn't leave a name and didn't want to be identified. When it turned out to be a real call and not a prank, nobody bothered to track the call."

"So there's nothing in the report about how Peterson got ashore?"

"Nothing."

"Can I talk to this Landon or Becker?"

Another beat of silence.

"Well, neither one works here anymore."

A dead end. But Keira didn't want to give up.

"Any idea where I can find them?"

"I'm pretty sure Becker took some job with a mining company in South America. Landon, though, she took a dispatcher job over at Coventry."

"Coventry?"

"Another ambulance service north of here."

"Thank you. This is very helpful."

"Who did you say you were with?" the woman asked.

But Keira had already hung up.

Chapter Thirteen

Having a lead to the mystery and possibly learning the full story suddenly scared the shit out of me. "Maybe this isn't such a good idea," I said.

Keira gave me a hard look. "Hey, you started this goose chase. Let's go."

"Go? Go where?"

"I don't trust another phone call. We should go find this Coventry place and this Landon woman and get the story in person. We'll go in my mom's car."

She wasn't thinking straight. Yes, she had access to an old wreck of a car, and it might even get us there. But I couldn't get in it. I pointed down at my heavy goddamn motorized machine that I was completely dependant on to get from point A to point anywhere.

"Oh," she said. "Then I'll go. You can run off to your next class like a good little student." She sounded downright angry with me. I didn't get it. But in a split second she was up and gone. I was left sitting alone in the library.

✦

I went to history and then math, and after that the Accessibus was at the school door, ready to take me to my physio session with Ahmad. I rolled into the room and saw he wasn't alone.

There was a sorry-looking kid sitting in a chair beside him.

"I brought someone to meet you," Ahmad said. "Nick, this is Ocean."

The name struck me as totally crazy. Ahmad saw the look on my face. "I know. Everyone here reacts the same way. Ocean is his real name. It's quite a common one in Syria, but you can call him O.C. That seems to go over better here."

"Hello," the kid said. "Nice to meet you."

I would say he was maybe fourteen, but he could have been younger.

"Hi, O.C. Nice to meet you." I turned to Ahmad. "Your cousin, right?"

"Yes. O.C. has only been with us for a few days. I'm trying to teach him the ropes. I wanted him to meet you, to get to know you."

Ocean looked me up and down.

"How's life?" I asked.

"Better," he said. His accent was strong.

"You understand English?"

"Of course. Lots of school time. Want to ask me something hard?"

I figured I had insulted him by asking about his English. Everyone he met probably asked him the same damn thing. "No," I said. "You like it here?"

"I don't know yet. Ahmad, Eva and my aunt have been kind to me."

"Me too," I said.

"How long?" the kid asked, nodding at my chair.

"A few months," I said. Like the kid, I wasn't keen on a lot of personal questions, I guess. I toggled the control and swiveled back and forth like a silly little dance.

O.C. smiled. "Cool," he said.

"Not really. It'd be much more cool if batteries and motors weren't involved."

"O.C.," Ahmad said, "Nick showed you his. You want to show him yours?" It struck me as a totally bizarre thing for Ahmad to say.

O.C. let out a little snicker, and I was thinking I should get the hell out of there. But then he pulled up his pant leg and kicked off his shoe. He had an artificial leg.

"He hates it," Ahmad said. "I keep telling him it just takes time. A lot of time."

O.C. glared at his cousin. "It's not just this," he snarled. "I don't think some things ever heal."

"The prosthesis is still new," Ahmad told me. "He says he prefers the crutches."

"I got used to them, at least."

Ahmad turned to me and started to tell the story. "Ocean lost—" he began.

"Shut up, Ahmad," the kid snapped, and Ahmad did. "If the story has to be told to this stranger, I should at least be the one to tell it."

I looked at the kid—a really angry kid now. "You don't have to tell me anything if you don't want to." I knew exactly how he felt. At least, I thought I did.

"What I lost was my entire family. Both my parents and my little sister." He paused and then pointed to his leg. "And this. An explosive buried in the road."

I didn't know what to say. Had Ahmad introduced me to O.C. so I could see that someone was maybe worse off than I was? If so, that really made me mad.

"What is this about?" I asked Ahmad. He heard the rising pitch in my voice. "You think *this* is going to help me somehow?"

Right then I didn't give a rat's ass about O.C. or Ahmad.

"No, damn it!" Ahmad was close to shouting, which surprised me. "I want *you* to help *us.*"

O.C. slapped his prosthesis and pulled his pant leg down. "I don't want his help," he said defiantly, looking straight at me.

That's when I decided I really liked this strange new kid.

Chapter Fourteen

O.C. limped off to a corner of the room, sat down at a computer and pulled up a video game. He set the sound as loud as he could and started shooting.

"How's he know about video games?"

"He knows about a lot of things. We weren't exactly cut off from the world over there. We were just caught in the middle of a conflict that tore our country apart."

"He's lost everything and wants to play a video game?"

"No, he wants everything to go back to the way it was. But it won't."

I looked over at O.C. He didn't look back. He was totally absorbed in his game.

Ahmad changed the subject. "Tell me about the pain in your legs."

So I was here for my therapy session after all. I told him about the rough nights I'd had recently.

"Did you hear from your doctor about having more tests?" Ahmad asked as he helped me move through my exercises.

"Yeah, but they can't get me in until next week."

"Then you'll have to hang in there."

We continued the exercises, but getting through them was more painful than normal. *Normal*. Huh.

"You got something for the pain?" I asked.

I smiled. He didn't like that. "Be careful," he said. "Don't overdo it. It's very easy to get dependent on the painkillers."

"Yeah, man, I know."

Ahmad looked at me for a long moment. "Okay, I think that's enough for today. Why don't I drive you home in the van? Ocean, c'mon. Let's go."

"I get to ride in the front!" said O.C.

I loved the van owned by the clinic. It was a step up from the old thing my dad had bought, with its noisy hydraulic lift that drew the attention of kids at school or anyone within a one-block radius. Ahmad guided me to the lift and let me pull the lever, and I went up, rolled into the open floor space and locked in my chair.

The kid looked a bit more lively as he started to climb into the front seat, but then he stumbled. He saved himself from a face-plant by grabbing the door. I could hear him cursing under his breath.

As we backed out of the parking lot, Ahmad put on some loud music—Middle Eastern, I figured. It had a pretty decent dance beat. Both Ahmad and O.C. sang along. Badly. I was an outsider, an intruder, but it felt good nonetheless.

When we got to my house, I asked O.C. if he wanted to come in to see my room, but he said, "No way." I respected that.

Once inside, I felt shooting pain again. This time it went from my knees all the way up to my neck. I downed some pills and waited for it to subside.

I got a text from Keira.

Found Landon. Can I come over?

Keira had never been to my house.
She was sure to freak out my mom.

Now?

Now.

OK.

Chapter Fifteen

My bedroom got moved to the first floor of my house after the accident. It had been my parents' bedroom, and I'd never quite felt comfortable there, but it made sense. My mom was upstairs reading in my old room when I saw Keira at the door. I rolled out and invited her in before she could hit the doorbell.

"Nice house," she said. "At least, a whole lot nicer than my place."

Keira, I had learned, lived with her mother in an apartment complex known to be the hangout of crack addicts and hookers. So I guess my suburban-bland split-level looked pretty good to her.

"Follow me," I said. I led her into my bedroom and closed the door.

She gave me a weird look. "If you're thinking of trying to take advantage of me, you are sadly mistaken."

I guess I gave her a weird look back.

"I was joking," she said.

"Not funny," I replied. "Not funny at all. But thanks for coming over. What'd you find out?"

"I took the bus to the Coventry ambulance place and caught the Landon woman when she was on break."

I had a sudden flashback to the paramedic leaning over me. Her face was clear in my mind now, even though I had not recalled much of anything about the ambulance ride until this moment. "I remember something. The last time I saw her, she looked worried. And scared too. I remember her hands were shaking. I heard her yell to the driver, 'Go faster. I think we're losing him.'"

"Him meaning you."

"What was left of me."

"She remembered you. She kept saying to me something about you being so young. 'What a waste.'"

The words had a strange echo inside my head. Wasted. As if what was left of me didn't matter. "How did they find me?"

"At first she was a bit fuzzy on the details. There was that anonymous 9-1-1 call telling them to go to the end of Fraser Road out by Delbert Point. When they got there, at first they saw nothing.

No sign of anybody. And then this crazy old man jumped right out in front of them. They nearly ran him over."

"The Wreck," I said.

"The what?"

"The Wreck. He's an old surfer who lives out there. His real name is Arnold or Arnie."

"Landon said he was crazy. Totally incoherent. She got out of the ambulance, and he grabbed her arm. She tried to push him away but realized he was leading her someplace. To you. On the beach."

The realization made the blood drain from my head. "It was him. No one else was around. He would have seen me in the ocean, seen me wipe out. He must have somehow got me ashore."

"And saved your life."

"Jesus." And then I was silent.

Keira studied my face. "What's going on?"

"We always treated him like crap. Crazy old goof. He was always lecturing us, telling us where to paddle out, where to sit, which waves to pick. He had an old dinged-up board and wore this patched old wetsuit. Lived alone in an old camper and seemed really paranoid of the police."

"Sounds like you owe him an apology."

"More than that. Do you have any idea what it was like out there that day? The waves, the currents, the ocean pounding over jagged rocks?"

"If it was so bad, why were you in the water?"

"To prove something to myself."

"Why do guys always have to say that?"

"I'd had some serious wipeouts before in big waves. Hold-downs under-water where you can't claw your way to the top. I thought I could handle it.

But when I went down that time, I hit bottom. It all went black. I can't remember a thing."

"Maybe that's a good thing."

"But I want to know. I need to know what happened next."

"Why?"

"I don't really know. I just do."

"Then we need to talk to this guy. This Wreck."

"Yeah, we need to talk to Arnie." I wheeled myself to my closet and grabbed a coat. I looked at Keira in her flimsy denim jacket. I grabbed another winter coat and threw it at her.

Chapter Sixteen

My mom had left the keys to the van in the bowl by the door as usual. I looked upstairs and saw that the light was out in my old bedroom. She must have been taking a nap. "Come on," I said to Keira. "Can you drive a van?"

"You mean that thing sitting in your driveway?"

"I bet it's a whole lot more dependable than that junk heap you drove to school."

"Screw you. You want me to drive or what?"

"Please. I want you to drive."

The hydraulic lift groaned and squeaked as it lifted me into the back. I prayed it didn't wake my mom. Keira had a difficult time backing us out of the driveway, but soon we were on the street, and I was directing her to Fraser Road.

Keira was a nervous driver, looking in her rearview mirror every few seconds. "If we get stopped, you can't let the cops get me for stealing this."

"I won't," I said. "Girl helps gimp. The police will buy it. They'll understand."

"Don't use that stupid word," she said.

Which was funny, because she was the one who'd used it first.

✦

Keira was no ace at driving but not bad considering she didn't even have a driver's license. She got us there. I remembered where Arnie's old camper van was usually parked—past the end of Fraser Road in a patch of low, wind-whipped trees half hidden from sight. The only problem was, you couldn't drive there in the van. There was a long patch of sand between the end of the road and his camper. No way could I get there in my chair.

Keira pulled to a skidding stop on some loose stones. I pointed her toward the stand of scrubby trees, and off she went.

I rolled myself to the back of the van, opened the doors and lowered myself onto the cracked pavement. Keira had disappeared from view. There wasn't a breath of wind, and it was dead silent.

And then I heard someone yelling. A man's voice in a high-pitched kind of scream. "Get out!" he said. It was Arnie's voice. The Wreck. The crazy old bastard we all had made fun of. We'd goaded him in the water sometimes if he was bold enough to surf in our midst. We'd teased him, bullied him even. He was a paranoid old dude and an easy target. We'd been jerks.

"No!" I heard him shout again. "Leave me alone. I don't want to see him. I don't want to see anybody. Just get out!"

I started to worry about Keira's safety. What if the old goon hit her or something? What good was I, stuck in my wheelchair? No way to cross the sand to where she was. I felt my fists tighten with frustration. Then I heard Keira's voice, as loud as his. No, maybe louder, more powerful.

"Shut up!" she shouted. "Shut up and just listen."

And then there was silence.

I unclenched my fists and squeezed the rails of my chair. I took three deep breaths and tried to focus.

I saw Keira walking toward me. The Wreck was right behind her, weaving a bit back and forth, muttering something. But headed in my direction.

Keira looked a little shaken but defiant. She stopped in front of me and rolled her eyes, then walked off to the side. The Wreck, Arnie, stopped in his tracks. His eyes were wide, and his mouth was open. He stared at me with a kind of crazed confusion, and then his expression changed.

"You," he said. "It's you."

"I-I wanted to thank—" I stammered.

"You wanted to what?" he interrupted. "You wanted to thank me?"

"Yes."

He looked long and hard at me now. Looked me in the eyes and then stared at my legs. He had a kind of maniacal half smile. Then he turned dead serious. "I didn't do you any favors, did I?" he snapped. Then, turning to Keira, he shouted, "Get him out of here!" He spun around in a circle and then spoke to the sky. "Why can't they just leave me alone?"

Arnie started walking back toward the bush where his camper was, shuffling his feet in the sand. But then he stopped, walked quickly back to me and leaned in. "And don't tell the police where my camper is, you hear?" he said threateningly. He clapped his hands once for emphasis and then tromped off.

Keira tried to stop him, but Arnie pushed her away.

"I can see why they call him the Wreck," she said as we watched him hobble off. Then she shrugged, and her tone changed. "I do get it though. He's scared. He doesn't trust anyone. Maybe he has a good reason not to."

"I can see that. The guy's always been a little nuts, but I still need to talk to him."

She nodded in his direction. "His camper—it looked like somebody tried to burn it or something."

I shook my head. "Someone is always trying to harass the poor old guy. Surfers sometimes, but the nasty punks from town are worse. They drive out here and try to spook him. God knows what he's had to put up with."

"But he said not to tell the police where he lives."

I laughed. "The police know he's out here living in his camper van.

They don't care. He doesn't bother anyone. They leave him alone."

"So what do we do now?" Keira asked, looking defeated.

"I will have to try again some other time. He's too agitated right now. We need to get the van back before anyone realizes it's gone," I said.

Chapter Seventeen

My mom walked out of the house as soon as we pulled in. She looked pretty upset. This spooked Keira. As soon as she shut off the engine, she tossed me the keys. "I'm out of here. I know an angry mother when I see one." She opened the door and hopped out without saying anything else. And then she ran.

My mom walked to the van and opened the door. She had a scowl on her like I hadn't seen in a long while. She helped me onto the lift and down to the driveway before she spoke. "Who's the girl?" she asked.

"A friend," I said.

"Why did she run away?"

I shrugged.

"Is she your girlfriend?"

"No. Just a friend."

And then she said a funny thing. "A *good* friend?"

"A real good friend," I answered. "And I can explain."

But instead of letting me talk, she leaned over and kissed me on the top of the head. "Let's just not mention this to your father, okay?"

"Okay," I said.

✦

I didn't sleep much that night. I woke up with an image of Arnie's crazed and paranoid face in my head. And then I had a dream that I was normal. That I was walking again. In the morning I had the familiar shooting pains in my legs and had to take some more pills.

Ahmad called my doctor and asked if the tests could be done sooner. I got a call and was told I could get them that week. "Don't get your hopes up too high," Ahmad advised, "but don't give up either."

I was beginning to think the therapy wasn't doing a damn thing. My upper body was stronger, sure, but down below it was all dead—except for those occasional shooting pains.

Keira was acting weird at school and didn't say much to me. "Problems at home," was all she said when I asked. But she was pretty cold to me, and I wondered if I had done something. I decided to just ask her outright. Her answer was right out of a textbook.

"It's not you. It's me," she said. "Give me some time," she added.

School days progressed sluggishly from one day to the next. Mr. Carlton had us reading and acting out this really long poem called *The Rime of the Ancient Mariner*. He said I did a good job of reading the parts about the sea and the waves and the monsters. I didn't understand much of it, but I knew plenty about the sea, the waves and the monsters. My monster was the fear that had dogged me in almost everything I'd done since that day on the Ledge.

Toward the end of one class, Mr. Carlton asked, "Why do you think the old mariner has to tell his story over and over?" And then he picked me to answer.

"I'm not sure," I said. "He's obsessed. He's damaged from the experience." I stalled after that. The words reverberated in my brain.

"Go on," he urged.

"He's trying to make sense of his mistake—killing the bird, which then led his shipmates into hell. He's trying to tell others not to do what he did."

"And that's it?"

No, there *was* more. But I sat silent and shook my head no. There was much more. But I didn't want to say it out loud. *The mariner was trying to heal himself.*

Chapter Eighteen

And I probably *would* be like that damned sailor in the poem, telling my own tale of woe. If only I knew the whole story. As crazy as that sounds, it was about the most important thing in my life—except for getting my legs back, of course. I needed to know. I tried explaining this to my dad, but he just said, "Forget it. Move on. Don't look back."

My mom was more sympathetic. "We just want what is best for you," she said.

I wanted to talk to Keira about it, but every time I texted her, she never responded.

I kept bugging Ahmad for my test results, and he said they weren't ready yet. My insurance coverage for the physiotherapy was running out, but Ahmad said it didn't matter. I could continue for free. I did more than that. I started hanging out at his clinic most days after school. A lot of the exercises I could do on my own. Ocean was there every day too, working as a kind of assistant.

One snowy afternoon when a client didn't show up, Ahmad made a strong pot of coffee and the three of us hunkered down by the window to watch the snowflakes coming down. It was a wet snow, so it wasn't really building up, but I really hated snow now.

It made getting around so much more difficult for me.

"Don't hate the snow," Ahmad told me. "It doesn't hate you."

Ocean gently smacked his cousin on the shoulder. "Nick can hate the snow if he wants to. We all have to hate something."

Do we? I wondered. I was afraid to ask who or what O.C. hated. He'd lost his family. He'd lost his leg. He had a right to have a hate on for a lot of things. But, like me hating the snow, there probably wasn't much he could do about it.

"Have the dreams stopped?" Ahmad asked. "The dreams about the wave?"

"No."

"Unfinished business?" O.C. asked.

"Something like that," I answered. I explained about going to see Arnie and how he wouldn't talk.

O.C. shifted in his seat and stretched out his artificial limb. He seemed suddenly animated. Something about the Wreck had touched a nerve. "He sounds like my grandfather," he said. "When the war started, he trusted no one. He pushed everyone away, became mean and mistrustful, even of family and close friends. Do you know what made the Wreck like this?"

I shrugged. "He's a loner. Kept to himself too much. People started treating him like a weirdo, an outcast."

"I want to meet this man," O.C. said.

"Fat chance of that," I said, but Ahmad was leaning into the conversation now.

"You only tried once. We should try again. I'll take you there. Ocean wants to meet your friend."

Friend wasn't exactly the word I would use, and I was about to say no way. No way at all. But just then Ahmad's phone rang, and when he hung up he said, "It's a sign. My only other client has canceled for today. We can go."

"Go where?" I asked.

"Go to meet this Arnold man. This Wreck you speak of."

O.C. was already on his feet.

Chapter Nineteen

It seemed like a really bad idea, but as soon as we stepped outside, the snow stopped and the sun peeked through the dark, heavy clouds. I expected this second mission to be a complete failure, but the craving to know how I'd made it ashore was still gnawing at me. In the back of Ahmad's van, I phoned Keira and was shocked when she answered right away. I told her what we were up to. "Do you want to come with us?" I asked.

"Absolutely," she said. "I'd love to have another chance to have an old crazy man scream at me. I'll meet you in front of the library."

"You sure?" I asked. But she had already hung up.

✦

The snow was melting on the road and sidewalks as we slowed to a stop in front of the library. Keira got in and sat down on the floor beside me, giving my hand a squeeze. I made the introductions as Ahmad drove on. O.C., of course, was riding shotgun.

"This is like a pilgrimage," Ahmad said.

"A necessary pilgrimage," O.C. added.

The only problem was that Arnie's camper wasn't there. There was only an empty space in the middle of the stand of scrubby shore pines. Keira and O.C. went to investigate. Ahmad stayed in the van with me.

"He's gone," Keira said when she returned. "There were more burn spots around there, like someone set fire to some old tires. A few trees were scorched as well. It looks like something bad happened."

"But look," O.C. said, pointing to some rutted tire tracks left in the sand and snow.

We followed the tire tracks a mile or so back toward town. They led down a paved side road to an abandoned military property where a radar station once stood. Sure enough, there was Arnie's old camper van. It was just beyond a chain-link gate that had been smashed down. Just outside the gate were two cars, tucked into the trees like someone was trying to hide them.

As O.C. and Keira hopped out of the van, I thought I heard glass breaking. Someone was shouting.

"Let me go first to see what this is about," Ahmad said, playing the I'm-the-adult card.

"No," said O.C.

With Keira's help, I was already lowering myself onto the slab of old concrete where the satellite dish had once stood. There was more shouting and more glass breaking. I recognized the manic screech of Arnie. "Leave me alone!" he shouted.

Before anyone else moved, I toggled forward and wheeled ahead as fast as my machine would allow. The others were right with me.

As we drew closer, I could see four young men, guys maybe just a few years older than me. I'd never seen them before, and it was clear they were up to no good. They'd smashed some bottles, and it looked like they had broken a side window on the camper.

"Stop!" O.C. yelled.

Arnie was standing in front of the door to his camper. He had a baseball bat in one hand and was holding it above his head. The four creeps who had been harassing him turned and stared at us. We kept moving forward.

"What the hell?" one of them said. He was holding some kind of metal bar. Another of his buddies had a hammer.

Ahmad spoke first. "Stop what you're doing," he said in that professional, formal way he had of speaking.

Hammer tapped the head of his tool against his thigh. "Who the hell are you?"

Ahmad didn't answer. O.C. was about to launch himself at the guy, but his cousin held him back.

"You okay?" I asked Arnie.

"Do I look okay?" he snapped, shifting his bat to his other hand.

"Leave him alone!" Keira shouted. We weren't really getting anywhere.

One of the guys laughed out loud, and another one snickered.

"I'm calling the police," Ahmad told them, taking out his cell phone.

"No!" Arnie shouted now. "Don't call the police."

The creeps laughed. "Old man doesn't want the cops involved."

Ahmad put his phone away.

"That's better," Hammer said, staring at me now. He walked forward and tapped the side of my chair with his boot. Nothing hard, but intimidating. "I'm trying to figure out what this is all about," he said. "I'm looking at a couple of uppity Arabs, a cripple in a wheelchair and a Halloween girl. Friends of yours, old man?" he asked Arnie.

"I don't know them," he said. "Now leave me alone."

I almost thought Hammer was going to call it off, but his other buddies were getting restless. "Goon squad to the rescue," one of them said and then took his metal bar and heaved it toward Arnie, missing him by about a foot but denting the metal side of the camper.

Hammer moved a bit away from us and then heaved his weapon at the windshield of the camper. The safety glass held.

Arnie just started swinging that bat wildly in the air, even though no one was near him. Out of the corner of my eye, I saw Ahmad take his phone out again. But I knew that even with a 9-1-1 call, the cops couldn't get here for a while. I inched forward, not knowing what I was going to do. Hammer turned and watched me approach, a big, ugly grin on his face.

"Nick!" Keira yelled and ran toward me to cut me off.

Hammer just kept on with that stupid smile as his three goons joined him. It was then that Arnie made his move. He rushed forward with his bat held high, screaming. Hammer turned quickly, ducked low and made a football tackle on the old guy, bringing him to the ground.

Hammer grabbed the bat and raised it. Ahmad and Keira rushed to stop him but were cut off by two of Hammer's friends. I saw O.C. arcing around them in an awkward run, but he tripped over something—at least, I thought he tripped. As soon as he was down, he started yanking on his leg, and then I saw the strangest thing. He pulled off his prosthesis, crawled over to Arnie and smacked Hammer hard on the head with his artificial leg.

Hammer fell off Arnie as O.C. struggled to stand upright on his one good leg. The other goons just stood there, slack-jawed. Hammer was still holding Arnie's bat. He lifted it as if he was ready to strike O.C., but he didn't. He stared at O.C. wobbling on his one good leg, and then he looked at Keira and me. Ahmad slowly walked toward his cousin. I didn't know what he had in mind, but he stopped when Hammer dropped the bat. "What a freak show," the guy said. "What a goddamn freak show."

I heard a police siren in the distance. It was faint, very far away, but it was a most welcome sound.

"Screw it," Hammer said and turned to his buddies. "Enough fun for one day." He nodded toward their cars, and they sauntered off as O.C. tried to help Arnie get back on his feet.

"Now you did it," Arnie said to Ahmad as he listened to the siren.

"I did what I had to do," Ahmad said.

O.C. sat down on the ground and pulled up his pant leg. Arnie stared down at him as he fumbled with putting his leg back on.

The siren was getting louder. Arnie had the look of a trapped animal. I rolled toward him and grabbed his sleeve. "Stay," I said. "Please."

At first he pulled away, but then, for a full second, our eyes locked. I recognized the pure fear in them. Right then I knew I had seen it before, although only for the briefest instant. I remembered it like it was burned into my brain. I'd seen that look in the old man's eyes when he grabbed me in the sea just as a massive pile of white water slammed into us both, pulling us under. I must have been conscious for a second or two on the surface before I blacked out again when we were pulled under. Arnie had been scared to death, but he'd had the guts, the skill and the determination to get me to shore. To save my sorry ass.

Chapter Twenty

When the lone patrol car arrived, a single uniformed officer got out and walked toward us.

Keira came and stood beside Arnie and me as Ahmad explained what had just happened. He pointed to the camper's broken window and battered sides and then at Arnie. I was still afraid

Arnie was going to run, but Keira had her hand on his arm.

Ahmad and the cop spoke for several minutes, and then the officer approached us.

"You all right?" he asked Arnie.

Arnie nodded, refusing to make eye contact.

"He's afraid you're going to tell him he can't stay here," I said.

The officer shook his head and asked Arnie, "You like it here?"

"Not as good as my old home," he said. "Can't see the waves from here."

"Then you should be back there," the officer said.

"You're not gonna tell me to leave?"

"No. Hey, this is government land, and someone might chase you off from here, but back by the point you're on private property. We heard from the owner a long time ago, a guy who lives in the city. He said he had no problem with you staying there. Go back and watch the waves."

The officer picked up his shoulder radio and called in to report that everything was okay. Then he hitched up his belt and looked at me. It took a second, but it sunk in. "You're that kid who had the accident out here last fall, right?"

I nodded. "Arnie was the one who got me ashore."

He smiled. "Damn. You were one lucky son of a bitch." Then he rubbed his chin. "I saw you surfing once down by the pier. You were one damn fine surfer."

"Yeah. Was," I said.

"Take care," he said. Then he reached in his wallet and took out a business card. He handed it to Arnie. "Call this guy in town and tell him I sent you. He'll fix those windows for ya. No charge."

And then he was gone.

There was an awkward silence after the police car pulled away. O.C. was having trouble adjusting his prosthesis, and Ahmad helped him get it right.

"I guess we should go," I said.

"No," Keira said. "We came here for a reason." Turning to Arnie, she added, "Nick needs to know what happened that day."

Arnie looked confused at first. "This kid scared the shit out of me." It was almost funny the way he said it.

"Scared me too," I said.

Arnie scratched at the gray hairs on his chin. "I'll make a fire first, and then I'll spill the beans."

He got a small fire going with newspaper and twigs, then threw on kindling and branches that burned brightly in front of us. We sat down on some old milk crates he brought out of the camper, and he told us what happened.

"I was watching the ocean like every other day. But this day was different. Big, mean, deadly waves. I'd gone surfing once on a day like that. Swore I'd never do it again. Did it that once because I was a young macho punk who thought I was immortal. But as you get older you learn that none of us are immortal. Stupid here didn't know that yet, I guess." He meant me, of course. The way he said it made Keira laugh.

"So I see this kid with his brand-new wetsuit and shiny board come running past my camper and start paddling out to the Ledge. Just him. All alone. Like it was no big deal. I got out of the camper and yelled to him, but I guess he didn't hear. He was determined, I could tell that.

"I got my binoculars and walked up the headland a bit so I could keep an eye on him. My hope was he'd get knocked off his board on his first wave, wash straight in and that would be the end of that.

"But no. Bozo here misses a couple of smaller waves and then starts paddling for one of the biggest, meanest waves to come barreling in here since god knows when. Worse yet, he catches the damn thing and makes the drop. Drops like a stone. Not a chance in hell he would be able to make the bottom turn.

"By some sort of miracle, he's still standing when he reaches the bottom of the wave, but now he has nowhere to go. The wave has reared up like a mountain over his head. I stopped breathing as I watched the massive lip of that thing come crashing down on him. Worse yet, I see the wave has sucked out over that big flat piece of rock on the bottom of the ocean, so there's no way for him to dive deep and try to save himself.

"When I saw him get hit by that lip right over the Ledge, I was sure he was dead. I said to myself that no way was I going to go out there. He got what he deserved. But when I saw his body come back up to the surface, his face down in the water, I couldn't just stand there. When he got hit by a second wave that tossed him like a rag doll and pushed him down again, something snapped in me. Here was someone's son who was going to die if I didn't do something." He let out a deep sigh. "I know what it's like to lose someone you love. My wife died in a diving accident many years ago. I couldn't save her.

"It was like my legs just kind of took over. I ran to the beach. I didn't have time to put on a wetsuit, and I didn't think I'd be able to stay on my board with those bloody waves, so I swam. I've always been a good swimmer, but the currents were hellish. Dove under a couple of waves that kept pushing me to shore but then got caught in a rip current that took me right to him.

"When I reached him, he was coughing up seawater and seemed to be conscious, but it didn't last."

That had been my one moment of contact. Me, briefly awake, to see the stark fear in Arnie's eyes.

"I held on to him as we got hit by another wave that dragged us both under. He didn't fight me. His body was limp, and I just held on. That wave pushed us out of the rip, but I had to swim on an angle toward shore to avoid the worst of the side currents. To be honest, I didn't think we'd make it. I thought about letting him go a dozen times. I wasn't even sure he was alive. You can't tell if anyone is breathing in a seething ocean like that.

"But I couldn't bring myself to do it, to let him go. Either we would both make it in or neither of us would.

"And then finally I was dragging him like a dead seal up the beach. I waved to someone in a stopped car. The guy waved back, and he must have called for help, but he never came down to the beach. I did what I could—it'd been ages since I'd had any training in that sort of thing, but I gave it my best shot. He was breathing, but that was about it. I was shivering like crazy and still scared as shit. I don't think I will ever forget what it was like in the water that day."

No one said anything for quite some time. "Thank you," I finally managed to squeak out. "Thank you for saving my life."

Arnie, the Wreck, looked at me, his eyes shiny with tears. The fear was gone from him now. The paranoid stare had disappeared. "You're welcome," he said. "Just don't do anything stupid like that again."

Chapter Twenty-One

Those tests Ahmad told me to have done didn't really show anything new. The doctor said the pain I was feeling was a good sign. Maybe. Or it could just be the phantom pain that amputees some-times feel in limbs that are long gone. O.C. told me he often feels a sharp pain in his right foot at night when he's lying in bed. He throws back the covers, half expecting to see that his lower leg and foot have returned. But of course they haven't.

So I stick with the therapy. My arms keep getting stronger and stronger. Pretty soon I'll be able to lift an elephant or bend steel bars like Superman. Ha! The ironic thing is that these muscles are my paddling muscles. I was one hell of a paddler as a surfer. If I hadn't been so strong, I wouldn't have been able to catch that killer wave. I might have just given up after trying a couple of times and paddled to shore. Instead I went for it.

I mentioned this to Ahmad one day, and he sat me down at his computer and showed me a video from an organization called Life Rolls On. Paraplegics like me learning to surf. How crazy is that? Maybe, just maybe. I don't know.

Ahmad has not heard from his father in a long while now. But he hasn't given up hope. He's talking about going back to Syria to look for him, but his mother and sister think this is a bad idea. Too dangerous. They don't want to lose him as well.

Arnie got his window and windshield fixed for free, and the police stop by and check on him now and again. He's no longer afraid of cops. And O.C. has taken to hanging out with the old guy on a regular basis. "He reminds me of my grandfather," he has said more than once. "We all need family, and I don't have much left." I think Arnie has told him one too many surf stories, because O.C. has gotten it in his head that he wants to learn to surf when summer rolls around again. "Look," he says the people will say, "there's Ocean in the ocean." Groan.

The school year is winding down, and soon summer will be here. No one is telling me I will return to normal.

The doctors say I may have already "peaked" in my recovery. I hate that word, but it keeps coming back to haunt me. "You may see some improvement," is the phrase my doctor likes to use. The truth is, no one knows what my future will be like.

I can hope for more recovery, hope that I might walk someday, but I have to accept that it may not happen. And if that's the case, I have to live with that. I'm not the "ancient mariner." I don't have to tell my tragic story over and over. Now that I've heard Arnie's version of what happened that day, I've been able to move on. Somewhat. I don't exactly know why.

Maybe it's just the thought of good people doing good things, heroic things even, despite the odds. Maybe that's it. Hearing Arnie's story released me from my anger. He had nothing to gain and everything to lose, and he still dove into that crazy sea and pulled me ashore.

Keira has been a bit distant lately. Problems at home. Her father moved back in, and he's dragging them down. She's asked to stay over at my house at least a dozen times to get away from all the fighting. I always say yes, and my mom has even fixed up a room in the basement where she can stay whenever she wants.

Keira's pushed me away, though, more than a few times, and said some pretty nasty things. I know it's coming from a dark place in her world. I can take it. I really can.

"It may not be all that you hope for," I tell her. "But things can change."

Things can get better. One day you're this. The next day you're that. Everything can change so quickly. Not even in just one day, but in one hour or just one minute.

Lesley Choyce is the author of dozens of books, including *The Thing You're Good At* and *Identify* from Orca Soundings. He has won the Dartmouth Book Award, the Atlantic Poetry Prize and the Ann Connor Brimer Award. He has also been short-listed for the Stephen Leacock Medal for Humour, the White Pine Award, the Hackmatack Children's Choice Book Award, the Aurora Award from the Canadian Science Fiction and Fantasy Association and, most recently, the Governor General's Literary Award. He lives at Lawrencetown Beach, Nova Scotia.